Winston entered every contest,
but he couldn't wait for the
final race — the big relay!

I can really move!

D1347659

Winston's brother, Wally, would rather read about races than run in them.

Fascinating!

Mrs Meow blew the whistle
to start the first race.

Winston won!

Winston and Spencer teamed up for the wheelbarrow race.

Next was the pie-eating contest.
Winston and Zippy had to eat as much
as they could in just one minute!

Winston did his best but only came in second.

After the pie-eating contest, Winston lined up for the egg and spoon race.

Eggs smashed to his left and right,
but Winston's egg stayed on the spoon
and he crossed the finish line first.

Wally knew just what to do.

Winston was all right, but he couldn't run. Who would take his place in the relay race?

It was Wally who volunteered.

Wally felt nervous, he had never been in a race before.

When it was time for the relay, the Schoolies lined up.

START!

Wally waited on the line for Spencer to pass the baton. Then, off he went!

Yes it was! Wally's team won.

It was the best sports day ever!